CHAPteR oNe

A n extraterrestrial alien maneuvered a disc-shaped spacecraft 13 kilometers high in the troposphere under the influence of alcohol and a combination of abused controlled pharmaceuticals with patient information leaflets scattered on the floor. The space vehicle hovered over an unlicensed brothel, popular among sex tourists in Roswell, New Mexico, and a laser altimeter emitted short flashes of asparagus-colored light. The pilot continued operating the laser altimeter and determined the height of surface features on earth.

The spaceflight commander emitted a

fragrance from an air freshener spray can before he exited the waste collection system and returned to the flight deck with a textbook used in the study of homological algebra.

The flight deck control center consisted of thousands of gauges, switches, levers, knobs, touch screens, and lights. The copilot helped the spaceflight commander operate the vehicle on his lunch break. Instead of eating in the galley, the copilot attached a locker tray with fabric fasteners to his lap and ingested thermostabilized food with flour tortillas in the glass cockpit.

Thirteen crew members exchanged annual reports and financial statements in the center of the spacecraft's wall-to-wall glass conference room. One of the crew members aboard the orbiter video recorded the chief of police of Roswell, New Mexico, strangling an underage prostitute beside a truck mixer drum, and two uniformed peace officers un-arresting a college student suspected of driving under

CULTIVATING THE DNA OF CRIME

A THIRTEEN YEAR OLD CHARISMATIC GENIUS GROOMS HIS CRIMINAL ORGANIZATION

ROY ALBERT ANDRADE

K1LLER

Cultivating the DNA of Crime
A thirteen year old charismatic genius grooms his criminal organization
All Rights Reserved.
Copyright © 2014 Roy Albert Andrade
v3.0

K1LLER, Inc. http://www.k1ller.com
The trademark, service mark and trade name (e.g., the K1LLER name) are owned, registered and/or licensed by K1LLER, Inc.

ISBN: 978-0-578-14000-1

Library of Congress Control Number: 2014938409

PRINTED IN THE UNITED STATES OF AMERICA

the influence of alcohol in exchange for a fondling during a routine traffic stop.

An organized crime task force seized roughly over three-quarters of a million dollars, hidden in 75-pound masonry cement bags from a 12-foot stake bed truck with 42-inch high hardwood gates, parked in the back of the cathouse, during their human trafficking and sexual slavery operation. The law enforcement officers murdered the pimp, madam, call girls, and patrons execution-style on the estate. The organized crime task force planted false evidence to frame slain patrons and women who performed sexual acts in exchange for monetary contributions.

A crew member aboard the disc-shaped spacecraft entered the vehicle's two-seat flight deck and hand delivered an 8½-x-11-inch sheet of paper to the shuttle commander.

"There are precisely 13 million dosage units of generic prescription drugs, sealed and labeled in hundreds of thousands of non-reusable plastic containers intended for Homo sapiens on this 4.5-billion-year-old planet to consume. Each dosage unit was counted by hand and are bioequivalent to their brand-name drug in the U.S stock market!" he stated.

The spaceflight commander assessed the information printed 3.1 nanometers in diameter on the 8½-x-11-inch sheet of paper and created a paper airplane out of it as the spaceship landed on a vacant parking lot. Thirteen crew members unloaded the generic prescription drugs at one of the world's most wanted drug lord's industrial warehouses in a rustic area as part of a consignment agreement and prepared for takeoff into the earth's atmosphere.

The copilot witnessed a meteor approximately 45 miles above the earth in the night sky hurtling through the mesosphere and said, "Check this out! It's a shooting star! I am going to make a wish!"

The spaceflight commander said, "I suppose you still blow out candles on your birthday and blow seeds off of dandelions to make a wish too, huh?"

Suddenly, the spacecraft puttered, and the interior lights dimmed. The copilot removed his helmet, the earth extravehicular visor assembly, and upper and lower torso assembly of his spacesuit. He meticulously examined the instrument panel in his liquid cooling and ventilation garment, then yelled, "On second thought, I wish we had a full tank of liquid hydrogen fuel, because we are almost out!"

The spaceflight commander realized the liquid hydrogen tank was nearly empty and hit the liquid hydrogen fuel gauge, and then said, "This is a practical joke, right? The extravehicular mobility unit is in the exosphere and approximately 666 kilometers above earth! We still have 13½ light-years to travel, and this clunker only travels 13,000 miles per hour! We need to do something soon, before *we* turn into a meteorite!"

One of the crew members rushed into the glass cockpit and skimmed through the index pages of a New Mexico tourist guide. He shout-ed, "There's a spaceport in New Mexico!"

The spaceflight commander spoke over the internal intercom system and sarcastically shouted, "Marvelous! Does anyone else have any bright ideas they would like to share be-fore we die?"

The rocket's main engines discontinued burning liquid hydrogen and liquid oxygen from the fuel tank. The spaceflight command-er powered the ion engines to consume the spacecraft's xenon fuel supply and operated the spacecraft at flight idle. The copilot with-drew a clear styrene vial from an emergency travel kit and patiently read the drug label shown on the container, then stated, "This should calm my nerves," as he removed the snap top cap and poured a handful of opioids into his mouth.

The space shuttle's internal alarm sys-tem sounded, and the spacecraft gradually came to a complete stop in midair. Then the disc-shaped flying saucer spiraled downward at phenomenal speed and exploded like the atomic bomb the United States Army Air Forces dropped on Hiroshima in 1945. A mushroom cloud evolved and reached a height totaling 13 kilometers. A detrimental sound developed, and I awoke in a bedroom I inhabited alone.

I experienced a mild case of diplopia. I observed halos around the ceiling light fixture and removed dried mucus from the corners of my eyes. I had fallen asleep with the television on and had viewed a made-for-television western film for a minute or two. An eminent movie star was featured in the motion picture and fired multiple rounds with a long barrel revolver at his enemies with a lit cigar between his lips. I cut the electric current to the television and the ceiling lamp with separate remote control devices, guzzled 30 milliliters of liquid melatonin, and dozed in bed peacefully.

I twitched at the din of rounds being fired and assessed the situation carefully. "I thought

I turned the television off, just a minute ago," I told myself. I held up the remote control toward the television monitor, but the TV was already powered off. I thought I was imagining things . . . until gunfire erupted again. I rushed over to the bedroom window and spotted a high-end automobile in the center of the cul-de-sac with the headlights unlit just a stone's throw away.

I don't know the invoice price the dealer received from the manufacturer for freight, destination, and delivery charges, or the manufacturer's suggested retail price either, since the full-size luxury car was in high demand and in short supply, but the registered owner must have paid a pretty penny on the purchase price, because the vehicle had an extended wheelbase and an iconic hood ornament that represented something malevolent.

I rubbed my index and middle fingers over my eyelids because I thought I was hallucinating, but, as it turned out, that was not the case, and I realized I was not imagining things either. The driver-side rear passenger stuck a 14.5-inch barrel out of the rear window and began tailing a wounded man prancing around in a fatigue uniform in Alemania's front yard. The gunman poked his head out the rear window gripping the broomstick of a 7.5-pound semiautomatic rifle with 30 rounds in the magazine and waved his hand at me as if to say hello with a black tri-hole ski mask covering his face.

A stroboscopic effect occurred inside the vehicle as a result of heat and spark, which the firing pin was responsible for creating after striking the primer of each cartridge that was automatically loaded into the chamber of the rear passenger's military weapon. An unprecedented number of artillery shell casings spit out the rear window of the vehicle and landed on the cul-de-sac's porous pavement like raindrops. The man was shot several times in the upper torso and dropped his handgun as he fell into Alemania's rosebushes an underpaid gardener planted a year ago.

Another gunshot victim injured in the shooting was also being targeted. He was impacted with a fusillade of gunshots as copper-jacketed bullets flew out of a stainless steel barrel welded by the assassin and silenced the man. The thunderous sound of gases escaping from the gunman's 14.5-inch barrel provoked every canine in the neighborhood, causing the dogs to bark and whine uncontrollably, showing signs of nervousness as the thunderstorm concluded.

The bedroom door struck the media storage rack, and four 12-volt halogen light bulbs attached to the ceiling lamp illuminated. I rued being out of bed, but, it was too late. The old man stood at the doorway and tapped the palm of his hand with a thick black leather belt with a shiny silver buckle. The pandemonium caused by the sounds of screeching tires, gunshots, and loud music lured him directly toward the bedroom window.

The old man knocked over the six-drawer dresser in the bedroom on purpose and grinned at 21 vintage baseball cards in clear plastic polypropylene card sleeves on the floor. He shaped the vintage baseball cards into a ball and pitched the heavyweight cardstock at a poster of a world-renowned Mexican boxer pinned to the wall. The old man swore on his mother's grave I would regret ever being born if I continued associating myself with Alemán, a fellow classmate, especially, Alemania, Alemán's 32-year-old brother.

Alemania and Alemán's great-grandfather listed both of their names in an irrevocable living trust agreement he signed 4 years ago for estate and tax purposes before he died of an autoimmune disease recognized as insulin-dependent diabetes. He left behind liquefiable assets, such as municipal bonds, real estate limited partnership agreements, international stock funds, and other income-producing securities for a law firm to distribute. So, Alemania and Alemán abandoned their parents' luxurious $10-million mansion in Beverly Hills, California, and moved into a single-family house, previously in foreclosure, at the corner of the cul-de-sac after closing escrow.

The old man slammed the door as hard as he could after he exited the bedroom and yelled at the old hag at the top of his lungs for an explanation for not having an abortion. I had stolen the vintage baseball cards from a prominent comic book and trading card store in West Hollywood, California. I thought the trading cards would remain in mint condition as long as I kept them in the six-drawer dresser. I was wrong. I did, in fact, plead with Alemán to hide the most valuable baseball cards in a safe deposit box at the bank, but he thought it was a bad idea. One of the baseball cards was worth $500,000.

I hung out with Alemán and Alemania nearly every day of the week, even though the old man hated the notion. He knew Alemán's recidivism rate was as high as a satellite and that he was placed on probation for vandalizing a black-and-white police car on April Fool's Day. The old man was cognizant of Alemania's criminal background, which included a 2-year federal prison sentence, after pleading guilty to conspiracy to commit bank fraud, wire fraud, and mail fraud in federal court.

Alemania's legal defense attorney discovered that Alemania had been under federal investigation for over a year before he was charged for defrauding mortgage lenders by submitting to them misleading information, such as the borrower's employment and income, among other misstatements, back in 1991. The Internal Revenue Service conducted a financial probe and collected enough trial evidence to influence the jury's decision. Alemania was housed in a 68-square-foot single-occupancy prison cell for 2 years and complained about the birdbaths in his letters.

The numeric keypad to the home security burglar alarm system beeped five times in the hallway, indicating that the home alarm system is activated and operated by state-of-the-art technology. Aerodynamic noise surfaced the domicile, and the specific unit dispatched entered the cul-de-sac with the light bars il-luminated. I wrapped a silk-filled cotton blanket with an Aztec calendar-inspired pattern behind my back to avoid the delay of getting under the bed sheets, just in case the old man returned to the bedroom and rushed over to the window to take a sneak peek.

A helicopter circled around the barrio and provided airborne assessments of the incident through the departmental communications system. The initial responding public officer parked her vehicle beside the sidewalk and checked the condition of the victims. She scanned the cul-de-sac for potential hazards and waited for investigating officers and medical assistance to arrive.

I was unable to clarify whether the helicopter was decorated with LAPD decals, but the 30-million candlepower night searchlight was a dead giveaway. I speed dialed Alemán's landline number beside a pocket-sized mobile phone jammer from a handheld two-way radio and reached an automated answering machine. I left a brief message under a different name with the use of an electronic voice enhancer device and unloosened the tiebacks to the rod pocket curtains.

Fresno graduated from an accredited postsecondary institution of higher education in Quantico, Virginia, and acquired specialized training from the United States Marine Corps before the Persian Gulf War began. Somewhere along the line, he received, and accepted, an appointment by the president of the United States to become a marine officer. He became a second lieutenant and demonstrated his leadership skills to manage monumental military organizations throughout his career.

Months later, Fresno toured Japan with an officer's eagle, globe, and anchor emblem pinned to his fatigues uniform with a platoon of 40 marines. Fresno mailed me a 16-bit video game console and a shrink-wrapped retail product titled Chávez, based on the historical six-time world champion Julio César Chávez

Gonzalez. The video game publisher's distributor exported the goods to the United States with the aid of a customs broker to simplify licenses, duty fees, and taxes 6 months after its release in the Asian marketplace.

I had seen Julio César Chávez Gonzalez, one of the best pound-for-pound professional boxers in the world, fight other licensed athletes, such as Pernell Whitaker, Frankie Randall, Meldrick Taylor, and Giovanni Parisi on cable television. So I was somewhat familiar with the orthodox fighter's career and popularity within the professional boxing community. He maintained a record of 89 consecutive bouts without experiencing a loss and was recognized as an international superstar.

I disregarded the fools murdered in the shooting and entertained myself with the role-playing video game, Chávez, on the 16-bit video game console to kill time. I pressed various action buttons down on the controller and outclassed the computer with uppercuts, crosses, and jabs to the body. Sworn enforcement officers investigated the shooting as a double homicide, searching every nook and cranny for evidence in the cul-de-sac.

Our domicile had hardwood flooring upstairs a contractor installed incorrectly, which made an indescribable sound when stepped on. I heard footsteps approaching the Brazilian mahogany wood door to the bedroom and urgently unpowered the analog signal to the 36-inch tube television with the remote control. Unsurprisingly, the ceiling light fixture came on, and five brushed nickel ceiling fan blades began rotating in a clockwise motion in the bedroom.

"You are going to end up behind bars one of these days!" the old man stated, and dragged me across the textured polypropylene carpet. He held my face against the window, until water vapor condensed on the interior surface of the transparent glass material, and shouted, "People are shot and killed every 17 minutes. That's an average of 588 murders a week in the United States. Do you want to be part of those statistics?"

It was a rhetorical question. I remained silent and allowed him to win his frivolous argument without crossing swords with him. I recognized a thick leather belt in the old man's right hand and literally became hypnotized within a matter of milliseconds. An episodic memory reconstructed, and I envisioned past events I would never forget.

I had the intellectual ability to attain high scores in a publicly funded educational institution in Burbank, California. However, I used the 3-pound organ to design architectural drawings in a sketchbook to fulfill aspirations, and did not make a conscious effort to comprehend the material covered in class. As a result, I was not in high academic standing with the school. Alexander Graham Bell, Albert Einstein, Thomas Edison, and Walt Disney encountered the same problem in traditional schooling. So, I did not feel doltish.

I would relax in the dining room watching

black-and-white reruns of *Gilligan's Island* with bite marks in a half-eaten peanut butter and jelly sandwich and wait for a straight-A student to knock on the door after school so I could copy her homework. My grandparents ensured I was fed three square meals a day, wore designer clothes, was convivial at all times, and arrived at school 5 minutes before the morning bell rang.

A student progress report form wound up in the old hag's mailbox, which revealed I was on the borderline of passing—or flunking—the fourth grade. She literally drove 9 miles from Pacoima to Dr. David Burbank's old acreage, not to encourage me to do better in school, but to remind me of the old man's full-grain leather belt. The old hag imprinted a figure of the leather belt on the buttocks and lower back more than enough times to see red blood cells seep through capillaries.

The cerebrum reconstructed mental images of a buttocks, a thick black leather belt, and signs of hypovolemia. The old man rambled about God knows what and didn't look too happy. My eardrums failed to vibrate and pick up the sound waves produced by the old man's speech organs. I was puzzled and unconsciously assessed the motion of his lips for general suggestions of visual speech. I was incompetent at lip reading and remained silent.

Suddenly, the eighth cranial nerve began carrying nerve impulses from my ears to the brain. "Have you seen enough? Answer me!" the old man shouted.

I undecidedly stated, "No! I mean, yes," and backed away.

I peered out of the translucent glass window and recognized yellow resilient plastic barricade tape reading, POLICE LINE—DO NOT CROSS—CRIME SCENE, in black capital letters webbed across the cul-de-sac to cordon off the area. An investigating officer contacted the senior coroner's investigator, and a coroner's representative was dispatched. Investigators collected gunshot residue samples from the deceased, and documented the presence of any marks, scars, and tattoos.

The initial responding officer documented the identities and arrival time of rescue personnel, then directed them to the homicide victims. A public officer in an authorized long-sleeved uniform figured any of the suspects could have been transported for medical treatment and immediately called for patrol units to be dispatched to three area medical facilities. Another public officer limited access beyond the crime-scene tape at the entrance of the cul-de-sac, and recorded the identity of the prosecuting attorney as she entered the crime scene.

An on-scene criminal investigation division investigator arranged for a thorough crime-scene search and processed evidence for latent fingerprints. Everywhere the investigator pointed his flashlight, an evidence marker was placed next to a shell casing. I must have counted at least 120 evidence markers. Shell casings carpeted the street and caught the attention of the Bureau of Alcohol,

Tobacco, and Firearms federal law enforcement agency, because I spotted a man and a woman wearing navy blue field jackets reading BATF. A weapon defined as a machine gun by the National Firearms Act and attorney general of California was used.

The crime-scene technician developed a rough sketch to assist in interviewing and interrogating persons of interest. She dropped automotive carpet fibers on the ground to impede the focus of the investigation, and included evidentiary items on the sketch by triangulation. Blood collection kits, brushes, envelopes, and high-efficiency particulate air vacuums with special filters were used to recover, package, and stock evidence at the crime scene.

Another on-scene criminal investigation division investigator recovered a revolver and recorded the number of unspent rounds in the cylinder. Two bodies laying lifelessly on Alemania's front yard were being photographed and videotaped simultaneously as the deputy of the sheriff's Headquarters Bureau and lieutenant of the coroner's office fed information to an anchor and reporter from a local news station. The homicide investigation rested with the criminal investigation division as they broadcasted a description of the suspects and information related to their vehicle.

Both of the victims' fingerprints were taken and forwarded to the Federal Bureau of Investigation. I recognized our next-door neighbor with her arms crossed and nodding her head as an officer ordered her inside her haunted house. The bodies were covered with white sheets on a gurney and removed by an ambulance crew to be taken to the coroner's office to be examined by a licensed medical examiner.

The next-door neighbor is a block captain and refers to Alemania as a troublemaker at neighborhood watch meetings. She hated loud music, and brought it to the attention of the police department. Alemania violated the noise ordinance of the Los Angeles municipal code and was issued a non-traffic notice to appear. Nearly half the time, rotating officers in mobile police units parked 150 feet from his property line. He thought very little of the block captain's police-community partnership and the city's residential zoning codes or else he would have dropped the decibel level to 50.

The Los Angeles County city attorney contacted Alemania one day and advised him to relax, because the city council was going to amend the noise ordinance to include a new sound level that would benefit him, so he could play his music even louder in our municipality. The homeboys spent hundreds of thousands of dollars to influence city elections and helped the former Assemblyman Florida defeat incumbent El Paso in the race for Los Angeles city attorney in 1994. Florida felt like he owed us a favor, and the city attorney's office revised the municipal law.

It was 12:59 A.M. I walked languorously to

bed and set the digital alarm clock for 7 ante meridiem. I became unconscious for the next 7 hours, and drooled on an orthopedic pillow as I dreamt of an airliner crash-landing upside down into an empty field, killing 247 passengers onboard.

CHAPteR tWo

I reached for an unopened box of breakfast cereal packed with fiber, whole grains, fortified vitamins, and minerals, along with a single banana from a 4-x-9 foot rectangular food storage walk-in pantry at 7:11 A.M. I used formal flatware to cut the yellow ripe radioactive banana into thin layers and mixed a little less than a gram of potassium in a 19-ounce military camouflage-patterned ceramic bowl with a silver spoon on a round cottage oak pedestal kitchen table.

I removed a chewy, warm, and gooey breakfast casserole with egg, bacon, cheese, milk, and seasoning ingredients from the microwave and munched on some jalapeño potato chips of incomparable flavor in the food products industry. Then I tilted the cereal bowl slightly over the kitchen table and gulped the remainder of low-fat milk with a multivitamin tablet containing various micronutrients. I placed the butter knife, spoon, and cereal bowl in the built-in dishwasher, and advanced to the vintage white arrow-back chair at the round cottage oak pedestal kitchen table.

I perused the text a professor of psychology and marketing approved to be printed on the cereal box's biodegradable material promoting a plastic-wrapped baseball card and fished out the prize in the petroleum-based product cereal box liner with one hand. The doorbell chime sounded, followed by a knock at the door. A peace officer and a homicide detective stood side by side at the doorway.

The uniformed police officer had his heavy-duty police badge covered with a black mourning band affixed to his stifling dark blue wool uniform above authorized military ribbons. The official department-issued badge had a border design similar to an ancient Roman symbol and sunrays over a replica of the city hall of Los Angeles. I stared at the city seal of Los Angeles, which portrays the city's history through Spaniard, Mexican, and European American oversight and laughed, because I had run into the badge more times than I care to admit.

I detached both brown eyes from the oval-shaped badge and concentrated on his workmate, the homicide investigator, who had mentioned he wanted to follow up on a preliminary investigation and report that was submitted by the initial responding law enforcement officer from yesterday's deadly shooting. The purpose of their follow-up interview is to gather supplementary evidence and intelligence to validate the elements of the double homicide in order to make an arrest and back up prosecution of the suspects. Like I cared!

The homicide investigator had a neatly trimmed jet-black mustache and a daunting scar beside his left eye. He took one last drag of his high-quality-brand cigarette as the filter's cellulose acetate trapped carcinogenic chemicals, and then he used the sole of his exotic western boot to smash the cigarette butt on the front porch brick paver. This dude was wearing a three-piece single-breasted business suit and a nicely shaped western felt hat that perfectly matched his personality.

I paid close attention to the sleuth covered in extraordinary garments and his fashionable rich 8-ply silk designer necktie as he battled to pronounce every word he conveyed in American English. Nonetheless, I disregarded his authentic Mexican Spanish accent and figured out precisely what he was trying to say as he used a portable radio to communicate, in code, with a patrol unit in the cul-de-sac. I knew he was in the business of preparing evidence for courtroom presentations and relevant reports for the district attorney's office, so, breaking silence was going to be his Achilles' heel, not mine!

The middle-aged man guised in opulent businesslike attire introduced himself as Sherlock Holmes, a Police Detective II, and his colleague as Watson, a Police Officer II, from the Los Angeles Police Department. I had seen Sherlock Holmes and the detective trainee before, but didn't know where, and gave the sworn police officers the benefit of the doubt that they were not going to waste my time, because there were financial news programs produced for prime-time broadcast I would prefer to watch, and video games to play.

"The proliferation of deadly weapons in recent months has made drug violence in America deadlier," Sherlock Holmes stated . . . and continued running his mouth. I immediately thought of street-level drug markets, black tar heroin, withdrawal symptoms, epileptic seizures, hepatitis B, multiculturalism, jurors, lay witnesses, acquired immune deficiency syndrome, corpus delicti, poppy plants, overdoses, morphine, colorful balloons, cash, collapsed veins, and riposted, by saying, "Are you sure you have the right house?"

Acts carried out by sworn police officers operating above and beyond the ceiling of their lawful authority was nothing new in Los Angeles. It's called Color of Law abuse. I could not have expounded the Constitution of the United States that the members of the Constitutional Convention signed on September 17, 1787, or the first 10 amendments of the Bill of Rights, and was uncertain if they were acting under Color of Law or violating a police misconduct statute. On the contrary, I knew I had the right to remain silent and right to legal counsel. I didn't panic. After all, it was just an interview.

According to Florida, a public officer could not interrogate a suspect more than 6 hours because of the 6-hour rule. Plus, it would be considered an inherently coercive interrogation and automatically involuntary. My rights were guaranteed by *Miranda v. Arizona*, 1966, thanks to Ernesto Miranda. However, their noncustodial interview did not necessitate that they read the Miranda admonition verbatim in order to use any statement I made as evidence in court or apprehend the suspects involved in yesterday's gunfight.

"Is your name Killer?" Sherlock Holmes asked.

I hesitated to respond, and said, "Sir, yes, sir! That's the name that's printed on a birth certificate I have upstairs and maintained by the California Department of Public Health Vital Records, sir."

Sherlock Holmes replied, "We are not obligated to delay our administrative investigation for a custodial parent prior to questioning you. Although this may reign true, is there a parent, legal guardian, or anyone the age of 18 or older available right now?"

The old man inadvertently pushed me aside and said, "Good morning, Officers! How can I help you?"

Watson furtively elbowed his coworker, Sherlock Holmes, and stated, "Well," and turned his attention over to his partner in crime.

Sherlock Holmes rubbed the palms of his hands together and said, "A drive-by shooting occurred Friday evening at approximately 9:59 P.M., which left two Hispanic males face flat for a highly trained team of emergency medical technicians to transport to the coroner office's homicide room."

"Are you trying to tell us our lives are in danger?" the old man said in a distressed tone of voice.

Sherlock Holmes shook his head and said, "No! No! No! Our two-officer patrol teams responded to Friday's deadly shooting over the police radio and preserved as much direct evidence, circumstantial evidence, and DNA evidence as they possibly could for our department's investigative specialists, but failed to obtain any kind of intelligence from anyone living in your household."

"The coroner will release both of the victims' bodies for a funeral after they finish the postmortem examination," Watson stated, and began laughing hysterically.

Sherlock Holmes opened his alimentary canal and chattered about the unsolved double-homicide victims killed. He paused to catch his breath and mopped his brow with an ivory silk handkerchief. I envisaged the sworn police officers perverting the course of justice and submitting a follow-up report form to their commanding officer.

"To let you in on some of the details, Sherlock Holmes and I interviewed an exiguous number of residents that our specialized investigative division has identified as onlookers to Friday evening's deadly double shooting. According to your neighborhood watch block captain, your son can lead us to the apprehension and conviction of the suspects wanted in our unsolved double-homicide case," Watson stated.

"We would like to ask your son a few simple

questions to help us solve the 994th gang-related homicide this year in Los Angeles County before it becomes another issue for our cold case homicide unit to solve. We re-interviewed your neighbors and counteracted changes to their stories. We have reason to believe Killer may know something we don't," Watson stated.

Sherlock Holmes sneezed twice and said, "Your son may serve as a cooperative witness in our crime-scene investigation and aid in providing testimonial evidence that may be used to convict the suspects in future criminal court proceedings. There are a number of complications police encounter with cooperative witnesses during interviews, such as failing to build rapport, querying numerous closed questions, and disrupting them during their narratives. I want to tailor questions compatible with Killer's mental representation of Friday night's double homicide."

"Two high school students died on your neighbor's driveway yesterday. One of the victims was a student-athlete superstar with a 3.8 grade point average, and in the process of pursuing a higher education with a full-ride football college scholarship," Watson stated.

"All of that is over now, thanks, presumably, to a carload of heartless hooligans with nothing better to do but commit drive-by shootings and annihilate rival gang members, such as the ones discovered on your neighbor's property. The double homicide may be drug-related or involve an under-the-table bidding war among recruiters from top-tier universities, but we are making a precarious assumption that Killer can provide us with some credible information," Sherlock Holmes said.

The old man stated, "Is he in any kind of trouble, or is there anything else I should know about before we continue?"

Watson conspicuously gazed at his colleague's western stingray boots and stated, "Absolutely not," as he nodded his head. He continued by enunciating, "According to department entities and various government agencies, your son does not have an arrest warrant on file. You have nothing to worry about."

A section of the California Welfare and Institutions Code crossed my mind. So did the Gladys R. questionnaire that needs to be completed prior to filing a criminal case with the district attorney's office. The old man probably thought I was going to report him for child negligence and endangerment to the investigating officers during their field stop because he stood in the middle of the doorway and was acting funny. Child physical abuse contributes to malformation of the brain, antisocial, and violent behavior. However, I preferred to remain mute.

I never reported any type of abuse to the Los Angeles County Department of Children's Services, so why would I now to department personnel? I thought to myself. I did not want to end up in a licensed foster home or group home, so I had to shake off the pain like a world boxing champion and wear sleeves extending from the shoulder to wrist to cover visible injuries. Positive parenting skills to meet physical and emotional needs were nonexistent. A parent-child relationship was unimaginable.

"You are being accommodated with more information than we are receiving, and would be more than grateful if you acquiesce and let us to speak to Killer in a more secluded area," Watson said politely.

Sherlock Holmes smirked and stated, "This is a noncustodial interrogation, also called an interview, and does not require us to read Killer his Miranda rights. This should take no longer than 13 minutes for us to complete."

The old man rubbed the palms of his hands over his eyes and in a distressed tone of voice said, "Maybe I should search the phone directory for a prestigious law firm in the San Fernando Valley and make an appointment to speak to a legal advisor before Killer answers one of your questions."

Sherlock Holmes unloosened his necktie

and unbuttoned his suit jacket as his sweat glands released salty liquid, cursing his fashionable work attire with a despicable odor. He removed his handkerchief from the upper welt pocket and wiped his face completely dry. He shook his head in disbelief and said, with both hands on his hips, "I can complete an affidavit for a search warrant and submit it to our supervisor for approval with advocating documentation."

The old man was insulted and shrieked, "This is nonsense! You do not have a valid search warrant, arrest warrant, and cannot interview Killer unless he is in police custody and is judiciously suspected of participating in a criminal offense!"

Sherlock Holmes snickered and explained, "If the magistrate concludes that probable cause exists, he or she will issue the warrant and impel us to complete a tactical plan report form, which is basically a search warrant aimed at third-party records, such as telecommunication companies and depository institutions to obtain telephone bill information and bank records, if that means getting the job done!"

Sherlock Holmes anchored his hands beside his posterior thigh muscles from inside the pockets of his pants and his single-breasted jacket opened slightly for a brief second as a result. I took one good look at the police badge and mini flashlight attached to his belt. I made a conscious decision to memorize his designation of rank and department. His vertical shoulder holster was constructed of premium cowhide and concealed a revolver with a six-round capacity.

Sherlock Holmes had emerald cut canary diamond pentagon cufflinks, outlined with 13 carat total weight white diamonds pinned to the ornamental border of his sophisticated machine washable white long sleeve dress shirt. The sun's ultraviolent rays increased the reflection of light from the facets and augmented the brilliance, dispersing a bluish glow and white sparkles. I overlooked

Sherlock Holmes's western business attire and could not help myself but to complement his exotic western boots.

Watson's 15 facial muscles contracted, and he began laughing like a hyena. Sherlock Holmes didn't think it was funny and spit chewing tobacco on Watson's black, plain, tiptoe center-laced-style shoe on their tour of field duty. I broke silence and stated, "Did you know the skins of stingray species are 10 times more durable than cowhide? And that stingrays have small glands at the base of their interlocking jawlike teeth that contain lethal poison?"

"I enrolled in a foundational course taught by a molecular and cellular biology faculty member in an undergraduate education pro-gram as an elective. That is as much as I know about biology," Sherlock Holmes calmly stated and eyeballed the old man. "When the time is ripe, I will place Killer under arrest and have him interrogated by an expert interrogator at headquarters."

The old man refused to cooperate and said, "I hope you gentlemen had a wonderful time, but I must skedaddle. I have to work too, you know? Remember to bring a valid search warrant the next time you knock on my front door so you guys can sniff around the house for clues."

The old man slammed the door and shook his head in distress. The doorbell rang three times, and he shouted, "What now?" He reopened the door and was handed a written order commanding the public officers to search and seize objects in a specified place, and bring the same objects before the magistrate. The old man escorted the public-sector employees to the kitchen and served them a cup of fresh-roasted Mexican coffee the old hag brewed.

"Before we begin, I would like to say that we are not here to make a field arrest. The shooting victims have been identified, but their assailants are still at large, armed, and dangerous. We just want to ask you a few simple questions, and then we'll be on our way. Got it?"

I nodded my head up and down and stated, "Yeah! I got it!"

Sherlock Holmes explained, "Do not be apprehensive! We are here to help one another! Honestly! Do you know what the United States Marshal Service's major duties consist of, and what their mission requirements are?"

United States Marshals and their deputies arrest the country's most dangerous fugitives—federal fugitives, international fugitives, homicide suspects, and gang members, but I shook my head sideways and stated, "No! I don't know! Am I supposed to know?"

Sherlock Holmes smiled broadly and said, "The United States Marshal Service apprehends fugitives, transports and manages prisoners, protects members of the federal judiciary, manages and sells asset forfeitures, serves court documents, and protects federal witnesses. If you are in hot water, now is the time to speak up. The U.S. Marshals provide 24-hour protection and can provide a new identification with genuine documents. I am required by California general statutes to apprise you prior to examining our photo spread that our investigation will endure regardless of whether an identification is made by you."

I had a gut feeling Alemania and Alemán's relatives would appear in their photographic lineup. Sherlock Holmes and Watson were seated at the round cottage oak pedestal kitchen table. They wanted to employ a photo lineup as an investigatory instrument to develop leads and conclusively help justice preponderate. However, their popular analytical practice was going to prove to be inutile. The suspects in this case were not going to spend over one-thousandth of a second in a jail cell, waiting for adjudication of a felony crime from any word I said.

Sherlock Holmes placed a portable voice microcassette handheld recorder on top of the round cottage oak pedestal kitchen table in plain view and leaned back in the vintage white arrow-back chair with a sinister grin. "Your participation is significant to the correct functioning of the United States criminal justice system," Sherlock Holmes stated. "Half of the photographs were seized from two gang members wanted for 187 California Penal Code murders as evidence through the execution of an arrest warrant issued by the office of the Los Angeles district attorney and are being used by the Los Angeles Police Department and federal investigative agencies for identification purposes."

I knew a thing or two about the drive-by shooting, but wasn't going to make incriminating statements supporting the elements of the crime. However, Sherlock Holmes and Watson derailed from the motif and began babbling about molecules. Watson stated, "Two or more atoms that annex make up an atom. An electron microscope is required to gawk at molecules, because molecules are so diminutive."

Sherlock Holmes stated, "The first molecules formed roughly 15 million years ago."

Watson added, "The blue marble was structured approximately 4.5 billion years ago and was made particularly of ponderous molecules. For example, iron. Scientists can manufacture new classifications of molecules in biochemistry laboratories. One of the most popular molecules scientists manufacture are plastics. Hydrocarbon molecules also make up plastic and—"

Sherlock Holmes interrupted Watson and explained, "Look at this photo! There are over a dozen criminal suspects wanted by various federal and local government agencies in the photograph!" He pointed his index finger at a particular person exposing white LA capitalized letters in raised embroidery on a wool-woven royal blue major-league baseball cap and said, "This man owns a global plastic manufacturing company that provides produce bags, meat bags, and grocery bags with hippo handles at notable grocery stores worldwide."

I shrugged both shoulders, heightening them quickly and empathetically. "So?" I said. "Good for him!"

Watson focused on an idea with his eyes averted to the portable voice microcassette handheld recorder and stated, "Natural memory imperfections may lead to the misidentification of a 'might-be' perpetrator. In 1989, the first deoxyribonucleic acid exoneration was recorded. The federal government has passed laws to remunerate people who have been acquitted by post-conviction deoxyribonucleic acid testing."

The Los Angeles district attorney's office would mail me a lineup order letter to attend a live lineup and a subpoena to appear in court to provide testimony, if, I participated in their investigation and identified outstanding suspects. They had a hunch I recognized a few faces in the photographic lineup because the block captain swore on her great-grandmother's grave that she had seen us kick it together in the cul-de-sac.

"Confession contamination happens regularly. Look at the photo again. He is wanted by the FBI for unlawful confinement of a federal officer resulting in death. He has a surgical scar on his face and tattoos on his hands. Did you see this person commit the homicidal act, yes or no?" Sherlock Holmes said.

I shook my head and said, "No! I've never seen this person in my life!"

Sherlock Holmes pointed out another individual in a lustrous silk-woven shirt featuring a blue and yellow abstract print with a concealed-button placket, and said, "Do you recognize this filthy scumbag standing on the mill finish footboard in the second aisle of the 10-row aluminum park bleacher? His name is España."

I shook my head and said, "No! I don't!"

Sherlock Homes replied, "He is wanted by the FBI for first-degree murder and a humungous real estate-related fraud scheme. His whereabouts are unknown."

"Well, I don't know where he is at," I gloated.

Sherlock Homes explained, "Take a closer look at the underage person next to him on his right-hand side on the anodized aluminum seat plank. Did you see this person commit the homicidal act, yes or no?"

I shrugged both shoulders and said, "Nope!" I was wearing a royal blue acrylic beanie and a collarless ghost white T-shirt in the photograph. There was no way these clowns were going to identify me unless I gave myself up.

The U.S. Marshals had España on their top 15 most wanted fugitive list for the well-publicized execution-style shooting of a federal agent. Multinational law enforcement operations attempted to disrupt his cash flow using sophisticated investigative tools. Nevertheless, his business continued to flourish every second, and countless lives are lost as a result of strong business ethics day-to-day.

"His transnational criminal organization is answerable to insider commodities trading, wire fraud, false filings with the Securities Exchange Commission, drug trafficking, kidnappings, and murders," Watson stated.

Sherlock Holmes said, "Consumer protection laws guarantee meat products are nutritious, pure, accurately labeled, and packaged. Store-packaged ground beef should never be less than federal standards."

I knew where this conversation was going. España was not only wanted for his unlawful flight to avoid prosecution. He was also under investigation by the United States Department of Agriculture for adding more than 30 percent beef fat to hamburger-beef goods his privately held company manufactured and sold in interstate commerce, which did not comply with the Federal Meat Inspection Act of 1906, equivalent foreign meat inspection policies, and labeling regulations.

A law firm structured as a limited liability company filed a class-action lawsuit in a federal court in California on behalf of a fast-food-chain franchise owner, and all other similarly situated persons. The plaintiffs alleged España's U.S.-based multinational corporation's animal-based prepared products effects consumers' health and leads to serious health risks, such as high blood cholesterol, diabetes, and coronary heart disease. The food production company misbranded their products under federal law and was being sued because they claimed that its certain foods were of beneficial nutritional nature.

Psychological stress may be advantageous to some people. It may help them accomplish a particular deadline. On the other hand, psychological stress may make existing problems worse. España was transported in a private motorcade to a clandestine location, regularly, for his own protection, and carried his own blood supply to reduce the stress level. Military personnel stood at his shoulder, identified potential sniper positions, assigned him a code name to maintain secrecy in radio communications, and settled the question of personal protection.

"Over 35 million cattle are assessed every year on feedlots by the United States Department of Agriculture and Inspection Service. Meat is beef from 2-year-old full-grown cattle. Edible meat comes from breeds of beef cattle, such as Brahman, Angus, Charolais, and Hereford. The average annual per capita beef consumption is 64 pounds per person. Beef cows weigh approximately 999 pounds and yield an estimated 420 pounds of edible meat," Sherlock Holmes stated.

I was going to die of boredom and said, "Oh, yeah," exaggeratingly. "The chemical state of myoglobin in animal muscles determines the color of cooked meat. I had a close friendship with a cattle rancher. His name is San Antonio. He owns over 3,500 acres of rain-fed soil in various states and grows high-quality forage grasses to plump up his commercial livestock. Farming consumes nearly 70 percent of all fresh water around the world."

Watson stated, "What a coincidence! San Antonio is on the left-hand side of Colorado in the fifth row of the all-aluminum park bleacher!" He pointed at Colorado, and said, "Look!"

I laughed and said, "Colorado's name goes good with his red-rose-colored hair."

Watson moved his stirrer in circular motion inside of his cup of coffee and said, "San Antonio is a multimillionaire. He has a degree in animal science. Since 1964, his business firm has created hundreds of jobs in the U.S. and has managed its money good enough to realize a profit from day to day."

I applauded, and said, "He is in business as a commercial producer to produce beef for the nation's population to consume."

Sherlock Holmes asked, "Do you know how he started his business venture?"

I was familiar with San Antonio's biography and said, "Drugs!"

Sherlock Holmes said, "No! He borrowed $50,000 against the cash value of his life insurance policy."

I knew that and said, "A food inspector from the Department of Agriculture visited San Antonio's privately owned slaughter plant and discovered dentures among body parts scattered across an enclosure for 700 pound-wild boars in a secluded area."

Watson stated, "The case was not assigned to us to investigate," and laughed hysterically.

Sherlock Holmes said, "Never mind him. Does the name Polonia ring a bell? To some people it does, depending on who you talk to in each of the seven continents around the world. International staff writers, news reporters, and the like have written or spoken about him in newspapers, foreign and domestic television, and now, blogs, published on the World Wide Web."

I said, "You omitted receptors, codifiers, transmitting antennas, amplitude modulation, frequency modulation, receiving antennas, receivers, and speakers."

Sherlock Holmes said, "What are you talking about?"

I said, "You forgot to mention radio talk-show hosts."

Sherlock Holmes sat in his chair with his arms crossed and Watson stated, "Polonia is seated on the all-aluminum park bleacher right next to Alemania. He is married to Alemania's sister."

Watson stared at the kitchen tile mural of a stone terrace sculpted with Virginia creeper berries, a champagne-fruit-and-gourmet gift basket overlooking an impressionist landscape, and said, "We are working on an age-enhanced photograph of Polonia based on a booking photo dating back to 1990. He owns a private label bottling company that produces purified water for club stores and wholesale customers. I don't know much about reverse osmosis, do you?"

I hastily stated, "Reverse osmosis is one of the steps that makes desalination achievable! Speaking of the clear, colorless, tasteless, odorless liquid, there are over 1 million miles of long-distance water supply pipelines and aqueducts in America and Canada, ample to encircle the world 40 times."

"He was sentenced to 11 years in prison for soliciting the murder-for-hire of the government inspector assigned to his water bottling plant in Nashville, Tennessee, and fined $250,000. Polonia escaped from an administrative security metropolitan correctional facility in San Diego, California. He was discovered missing amid an afternoon count of inmates on October 29, 1990," Sherlock Holmes stated.

Watson asked, "Did you see Polonia commit the homicidal act, yes or no?"

I told him, "No."

Sherlock Holmes said, "Look at Colorado closely. He owns offshore rigs, tugs, fishing vessels, and an exiguous number of stock in publicly traded companies."

I paused for a moment, and said, "Huh! Now that I think about it, a government spokesman told television networks that the Federal Bureau of Investigation and Laredo, Texas, police are investigating a deadly shooting involving border patrol agents and one of seven gunmen. Officials requested the government of Mexico transmit Colorado's fingerprints to compare them to the gunman found inside a sports utility vehicle riddled with bullet holes."

Watson stated, "Colorado is in his late 30s, a native of Guadalajara, Jalisco, Mexico, and presides over a $500 million drug empire. He was arrested on April 1, 1989, in Little Rock, Arkansas, on charges related to drug trafficking, money laundering, murder, and sentenced to a 200-year prison term. However, he escaped from a medium security federal correctional institution in Forrest City, Arkansas, allegedly with the help of prison employees."

"So, you did not see Colorado commit the homicidal act, right?" Sherlock Homes asked.

"No," I said.

"Then who did you see?" Sherlock Homes asked again.

"I didn't see anyone," I responded.

"Are you sure?" Sherlock Homes probed.

"Yeah, I am sure," I said. I stood up, and Sherlock Holmes revealed a photo of Aleman in the stand-up cabin of Francia's corporate jet. I sat back down and said, "Why, am, I not surprised?"

"Aleman is Francia's cousin," Watson stated.

"Francia! I . . . I seen him on television. There is a reward up to $5 million leading to his arrest or conviction. He is wanted for violent crimes in aid of racketeering and con-tinuing a criminal enterprise among alleged federal drug violations," I said.

"Drug Enforcement Administration special agents and local law enforcement agents executed a search warrant 24 hours ago. They arrested 31 individuals, seized over $76 million in cash, and over 18 million packages of finished designer synthetic drugs in a manufacturing warehouse in the central business district of Los Angeles, California. Francia is the sole owner of the industrial property. He is considered armed and dangerous," Sherlock Holmes stated.

Watson chortled gleefully and said, "Not surprisingly, the deputy chief of criminal investigation at the Internal Revenue Service in Washington, District of Columbia, and an aviation enforcement agent, and marine interdiction agent from San Ysidro Customs and Border Protection field operations office were among those arrested. Rewards are obtainable at the absolute discretion of the United States Marshal Service for Francia's arrest."

I said, "Sounds like he is becoming an oligopoly."

Watson asked, "Do you know his brother's prison identification number?"

I paused for a moment, and then said, "No, I didn't even know he had a brother."

Watson said, "His name is Afgano. He was arrested the first of January at a cocktail party in Beverly Hills, California, with 10 other people linked to several Mexican drug-trafficking organizations. They moved hundreds of tons of methamphetamine from Mexico into major U.S. cities and laundered billions of dollars in illegal drug proceeds."

I said, "North America's most widely listened to radio talk host commentated on the *United States v. Afgano* superseding indictment a few days ago. The judge of the court of common pleas granted two witnesses immunity based on the testimonial evidence they provided during the criminal investigation. Afgano was sentenced to the death penalty."

"These Mexican drug-trafficking organizations horrify the Southwest border and abroad with kidnappings, torture, executions, beheadings, bribery of public officials and witnesses," Watson stated.

Sherlock Holmes ogled at a glorious colored handcrafted peacock figurine centered on the round cottage oak pedestal kitchen table and placed a three-dimensional mechanical puzzle on the tabletop. "Have a crack at it," he said.

I solved the three-dimensional combination puzzle in under 2 minutes and said, "A Hungarian man named Ernő Rubik patented and invented the first cubed puzzle."

"Once you comprehend a few algorithms, the six-sided puzzle becomes easy to solve, doesn't it?" Watson cheerfully asked. I didn't answer him.

Sherlock Holmes pounded his fist against the tabletop and said, "These goons can be anywhere!" He held up a photograph of Colorado and said, "You can earn $5 million in adjustable gross income."

Watson flashed an official department business card and said, "Tell us what we want to hear."

I wanted to laugh, because Colorado and Francia peeked out of the tree house's two-track double-hung aluminum storm window's glass and screen in the backyard with binoculars. The tree house had a 700-watt countertop microwave, compact refrigerator with freezer compartment, and camouflage sleeping bags. I watched them climb down the ladder and head toward the concrete drainage ditch and said, "I don't have much of a photographic memory."

"That's quite all right, little buddy," Sherlock Holmes stated with a peculiar smile. "You are something else. Do you know that? You did a splendid job. You should be proud of yourself. Let's get the show on the road, Watson, we have a lot of work to do."

I jetted up the staircase and heard the front door slam shut. The old man stormed into the bedroom and shouted, "You're grounded!" He unplugged the television and exited the bedroom with the 16-bit video game console. I slid the closet sliding doors to one side and uncovered a .22 semiautomatic pistol in a shoe box. I had a 10-round magazine and prepared to gun down the old bastard. The more I tasted my tears, the more I hated him.

A metamorphic rock hit the bedroom window and rolled down the red clay Spanish-style roof tiles. Suiza brandished two $1,500 ringside floor tickets to a private telecast boxing event in Las Vegas, Nevada. I jumped off the roof without a second to spare and landed on both feet. Then I sprinted to an armored sport-utility vehicle designed with gun cabinets, gun ports, bullet-resistant glass, bomb detection equipment, and state-of-the-art technology.

CHAPteR tHrEe

A muscled-armed bodyguard drove us to Las Vegas, Nevada, in Suiza's recreational vehicle and stopped at the casino's valet parking stand. Checo unfolded a financial daily newspaper over his lap and said, "The business firm delivered solid results in the second quarter and produced excess capital in the marketplace . . . Operating earnings for 1994 were $3.23 billion, up from $3.10 billion in 1993."

Checo serves as a member of Blue Bank's board of directors, a financial services empire headquartered in Los Angeles, California, and helped build the corporation from the ground up. Blue Bank provides a spectrum of banking products and financial services to consumers and microbusinesses. For example, checking accounts, savings accounts, merchant accounts, auto loans, and mortgage loans.

Lukewarm water traveled through a white vinyl hose and squirted out of a RV showerhead adorned with round brilliant cut diamonds equivalent to the diameter of a 1995 Roosevelt dime. I removed skin-borne bacteria with a pair of unused sky blue exfoliating bath gloves and a 4.25-ounce blue moisturizer-packed fragrant soap bar recommended by dermatologists worldwide.

The sky blue exfoliating bath gloves and 4.25-ounce blue moisturizer-packed fragrant soap bar were registered with the U.S. Patent, and Trademark Office by Irlanda's intellectual property attorney. Irlandés was the chief technology officer of Irlanda's conglomerate consumer goods company and influenced the manufacturing of innovative products, such as toothpaste, toothbrushes, toilet paper, antiperspirant deodorant, shaving cream, and cotton swabs in uncertain economic conditions.

Irlandés tossed a clean, personalized, navy blue cotton terry towel over the three-part French stripe shower curtain, and said, "Here."

I stepped foot on an imported majestic tiger-patterned bath rug and dried myself off with the towel. Austriaco was on the phone line with the president of the world's biggest media conglomerate and said, "You're the president of the biggest pay cable network on earth and earn $20 million a year. . . . This is going to be the most successful heavyweight title bout pay-per-view event to date . . . Thanks for engineering the pay-per-view distribution and clearing the fight with the multiple-system operators."

Austriaco purchased a 32-acre coastal estate in Malibu, California, 30 years ago and used a home equity line of credit to start up his business firm. He laughed in the face of recession and made millions of dollars as an investor. He jotted down a few notes on a 9-x-5.7 inch college ruled notebook and joked about his $1.3 million writing utensil. "This is one of the worst investments I have ever made."

Austriaco exited the RV and borrowed the parking attendant's mobile telephone. A motorcycle with an all-titanium frame, 200-horsepower V-twin engine, and cutout muffler entered the valet parking service lot. La Brea removed his motorcycle helmet and said, "I am honestly precarious about whether the Nevada State Athletic Commission will withhold the heavyweight champion's manager's portion of the purse for the quick stoppage."

La Brea has international sports contracting experience and provides legal representation on behalf of the boxing promotion company. He arranged for all ring earnings and other types of remuneration earned by the heavyweight champion of the world in respect to boxing, sparring, and training to be divided and distributed in specified per-centages as expressed in a boxer-manager contract.

Austriaco returned the parking atten-dant's mobile phone, spun around, and said, "Who cares?"

La Brea laughed and said, "Santa Fe was sentenced to 36 months in federal prison and ordered to pay $3.5 million in restitution to the Internal Revenue Service for employ-ment tax evasion. He paid his employees cash wages."

Austriaco said, "Tax collection is the Internal Revenue Service's business, not mine. Since 1906, Vegas has demonstrated positive signs for business growth . . . Building a repu-tation on gratuitous violence linked to orga-nized crime and making regulators opulent."

La Brea glanced at Austriaco's hand-woven tan brown leather huaraches with rubber tire soles and said, "The gaming industry is subju-gated by publicly held business organizations.

They are answerable to their stakeholders. They are explainable to the U.S Securities and Exchange Commission and are regulated by a gaming commission with a magnifying glass."

Austriaco nodded his head in agreement and said, "By 1989, Americans were wagering close to $36 billion a year, more than the film industry, sports industry, amusement park industry, cruise line industry, and music industry business generated combined. Today is August 5, 1995, and we are going to earn approximately $187 million in net revenue overnight."

Austriaco placed his right hand behind La Brea's back and whispered, "The 220-pound undisputed heavyweight champion's cornerman is going to enter the boxing ring to disqualify him 60 seconds into the first round of the title fight in front an estimated 16,500 attendees on pay-per-view without threatening the credibility of professional boxing."

La Brea squeezed Austriaco tightly in his arms and said, "Whoever perpetrates any scheme in commerce to persuade, in any particular manner, a publicly exhibited contest, such as tonight's pay-per-view title fight, can be fined and imprisoned no longer than 5 years under the code of laws of the United States. When a Federal Bureau Investigation probe becomes a federal sports bribery case, call me!" He jumped on his motorcycle and waved his left hand good-bye as he rode away.

Unsurprisingly, we unloaded five royal blue personalized Paisley bandanna-enriched five-piece luggage sets and three large-size corrugated boxes in the casino's valet parking lot. Austriaco had a sententious conversation with the world heavyweight champion in the valet parking lot, scheduled to fight an up-and-coming fighter from Southern California, on pay-per-view programming in the hotel and casino's 380,000 square foot convention center.

Austriaco orchestrated everything at a London, United Kingdom, press conference 3 months prior to the night of the well-publicized telecast mega fight of the century. He threatened to kill the world heavyweight champion if he did not stage three knockdowns within 60 seconds of the first round. Last year, the heavyweight champion netted nearly $10 million after all of the pay-per-view receipts were counted. This time around, he's guaranteed a $12 million purse that could turn into $15 million, depending on live gate and per-perview buys.

Austriaco was copromoting the fight with San Francisco, a multimillionaire business mogul born on February 4, 1959, in Nuevo León, Monterrey, Mexico. He won a gold medal at the 1976 Olympics at the age of 17 and went on to win nine world titles in five different weight classes, generating hundreds of millions of dollars as an international boxing star before retiring in 1987. He owned and operated 13 franchised convenience stores outside the ring as a professional athlete and eventually became the chief executive officer of his own boxing promotion corporation before his early retirement.

I unzipped one of the royal blue personalized Paisley bandanna-decorated suitcases for the heavyweight champion and displayed 10 bundles of 1,000 notes of the equivalent denomination in 10 equal straps of 100 notes each. Austriaco negotiated to pay the heavyweight champion $4.5 million in cash as a bonus and an all-inclusive vacation package to Hawaii. The telecast fight would augment Nielson media ratings for the up-and-coming boxer's next mega fight and undoubtedly inflame his popularity worldwide through pay-per-view revenue subscriptions.

Suiza had morbid thoughts and said, "Our business associates are monitoring the casino with a first-of-its-kind aerial surveillance system and are integrating into mobile security deployment teams for our own protection."

Fénix acquired two hotel keycards at 4:30 post meridiem at our private check-in from a desk agent and waited for us in a nonsmoking poker room. She reached inside her $1.8

million grenade-shaped handbag handcrafted from 18 kt. gold, decorated with 3,500 diamonds made by seven artisans who worked on it for a total of 9,000 hours, and said, "Don't lose it!"

I held the keycard up and said, "I'll try not to."

Fénix said, "By the way, I made a block trade with your hard earned cash," and handed me a sheet of paper. "This confirmation statement reveals what I bought, the price, settlement date, trade, commission, and additional activity in the trust account."

I assessed the confirmation statement and said, "Where is the Committee on Uniform Securities Identifying Procedures number?"

She paused for a few seconds to keep her composure and wiped her eyes with her fingers. "The CUSIP are these nine characters of letters and numbers."

I gave her a kiss on her cheek and returned to Suiza with the keycard. "Explain to him that the account will be turned over to him once the custodianship comes to an end," she shouted among the clamor inside the casino.

Suiza positioned his index finger in front of his puckered lips and created a recognizable phoneme-hissing sound as air rushed over his tongue. "SHHHH!"

I waved my hand back and forth at Suiza and whispered, "Fénix opened a custodial account at a brokerage and banking company in Encino, California. She is liable for managing the account until I reach 18. I am taxed at the child's income tax rate," with one hand cupped over his ear.

We occupied the top floor of the hotel. The heavyweight champion beseeched Austriaco for permission to count each banknote the Bureau of Engraving and Printing provided and shrink-wrapped in bundles for us. Austriaco was prepared for any strange turn of events and requested for three associates to monitor the hallway. The muscled-bound fighter and his cornerman stood emotion-less at a submachine gun equipped with a 50-round, cylindrical, helical-feed magazine. He fell to his knees, "Please . . . Please . . . Please . . ." he said.

Colorado held a house cue underneath the ivory ferrule and brushed blue color chalk against the leather tip. Francia made the eight ball on the break without a scratch and said, "I won."

Austriaco pointed the 4.25-inch length barrel of a semiautomatic handgun at the back of the heavyweight boxer's parietal bone and said, "What do you want, again?"

He looked hopelessly at the decorative synthetic-woven polypropylene carpet and said, "A rematch."

"A rematch!" Austriaco said. "That's not what you're here for." Checo placed an electronic banknote counter capable of counting mixed denominations in any condition against the carpet cove base, and Austriaco said, "The bills must be placed in the hopper to be counted."

Las Cruces stared at the room number glued to the door with Blanco and Negro posted like Scots Guards at the Buckingham Palace.

CHAPteR fOuR

We walked past flyers stuck under windshield wipers, panhandlers, excessively decorated restaurants, alcoholics, commercial outlets, stray dogs, foreign tourists, chain smokers, gallery art exhibitions, street prostitutes, spa treatments, shoplifters, limousines, drug dealers, pimps, an auto collections showroom, crack addicts, amusement park-style rides, and unparalleled nightlife events on the Las Vegas Strip.

Suiza, Austriaco, and I ambulated to a 49-unit apartment complex with ground-floor retail space displaying eye-level storefront signage reading "retail space for rent" taped to each window on the corner of South Las Vegas Boulevard and Gass Avenue. An accredited management organization managed and operated the rental property for Suiza. The property management firm was preparing vacant units to ensure minimal rent loss and handling rent control issues.

Suiza stopped in front of a wedding chapel at the corner of Gass Avenue and used a rechargeable calling card for international long-distance calls to contact an associate from a graffiti-marked payphone. "We need to market more auto loans and motivate loan officers to promote auto finance applications at branch locations nationwide," he said.

Suiza socked the half-inch thick steel faceplate coin box right-handedly, and said, "Consumers are more than likely to default on private student loans, qualified mortgage loans, commercial loans, and personal lines of credit debt before a simple interest car loan. This makes simple interest financing more profitable than other types of loans!"

I arched forward to reach for high-quality purple-colored Cannabis sativa divided in biodegradable mini-Ziploc storage bags and restored the white cotton nylon knee-high sock just below my knee before swooping up a lighter that had fallen from my short sleeve, eight-button closure plaid pattern shirt pocket with a respected exterior embroidered logo recognized across the universe. I sold five out of six marijuana bags and earned $500 in tax-exempt income in less than 5 minutes.

I reached for a tactical folding knife clipped to the inside of a pocket underneath my garment and utilized its stainless steel blade to cut down the middle of a premium quality cigar of tobacco to refill it with unsold marijuana I preferred to smoke. A considerable number of psychoactive chemicals like delta-9-tetrahydrocannabinol made their way to my lungs before entering the bloodstream and to organs throughout the body, especially the brain cells' cannabinoid receptors, when Suiza shouted, "¡*Espere, un minuto, por favor!*"

He covered the electret condenser microphone with his left hand to cut off all acoustic communication and interjected, "Hey!" in his statement. "What are you doing?" he said with a confused emotion expressed as a facial expression. "Africano is reading real-time quotes, and I am trying to make an informed investment decision."

"What does that have to do with me?" I responded.

He replied, "You are smoking marijuana publicly like a pot-smoking tourist in Amsterdam, the capital city of Netherlands. I am a nonsmoker. What makes you think I want to breathe in secondhand smoke?"

He walked away and left the phone hanging from its armored cord reinforced steel cable. "Law enforcement agencies made over 500,000 arrests for marijuana-related crimes nationwide. Do you want to be next?" he asked.

"No," I answered. I functioned at a suboptimal intellectual level and squeezed the .22

semiautomatic's black pistol grips like a woman's hand down South Las Vegas Boulevard.

A self-employed commercial photographer forced a film pack in her instant camera until she heard a *click,* closed the film door, and stepped approximately seven feet away. She held the instant camera steady and said, "Say cheese!" She pressed the shutter button, and a 3.5-x-4.2-inch instant color print automatically ejected.

Austriaco said, "Here," and handed her a wrinkled $20 bill. She looked at the seventh U.S. president's portrait, Andrew Jackson, featured on the front of the bill and thanked him for his patronage.

I was shaking the developing photo when Suiza asked, "Why do you smoke marijuana?"

I placed the developing photo in a pocket to keep it warm and said, "For spiritual enlightenment."

He laughed out loud and said, "That's the funniest thing I ever heard."

A white-bearded homeless man with a yarmulke on the back of his head dropped a cardboard sign covered with misspelled words, vomited, looked at Austriaco, and asked, "Do you have any spare change?"

Austriaco said, "I was going to ask you the same thing."

Suiza was disgusted and said, "The most commonly cited attributes to homelessness in America are underemployment, mental illness, and, of course, substance abuse."

I prepared a strong rebuttal injected with anabolic-androgenic steroids and said, "You forgot to highlight that the national prevalence of homelessness is also linked to mortgage evictions, victims of natural disasters, single-mother families, runaways, and veterans of the armed forces."

Suiza laced his fingers together, turning his palms away from him, bent his fingers back, and said, "Alcohol and drug abuse enlarges the risk of homelessness. The short-term mental health effects of marijuana use entail memory impairment, brain fog, cognitive distortions, and difficulties in problem solving. Ethyl alcohol is a stupefying ingredient in beer and impairs brain function."

I placed both feet shoulder-width apart and raised both hands to ear level with the nonthrowing shoulder toward a shatterproof polycarbonate panel with a green background. I stepped forward, released an unopened 12 fluid ounce canned alcoholic beverage, and created the perfect gyroscopic torque, striking the internally illuminated street name sign like an arrow fired by a world-class archer. The hanging brackets caused the street name sign body to sway, and the 12 fluid ounce aluminum alcoholic canned beverage fell on the hood of the engine compartment of a two-seat convertible.

"I bought this [expletive] at a collector car auction for $8 million," the vehicle owner shouted. He removed his newsboy cap and massaged his forehead. Then he began shuddering, picked up the aluminum can, and urgently asked, "Do you know who this belongs to?"

I laughed and said, "*Claro que sí, estúpido.*"

Suiza said, "Hey! What did I tell you about our code of ethics and business conduct? Did you forget?"

The Anglo yelled, "On February 2, 1848, former U.S. President Polk's delegate and the State Department's chief clerk, Nicholas Trist, negotiated with Mexican General Antonio López de Santa Anna for the Mexican government to relinquish California, Utah, Colorado, Arizona, New Mexico, and Nevada for $15 million! So speak in English! We are not in Mexico anymore. We are in the U.S.A.!"

I responded, "Thanks to superior artillery! And by the way, the United States does not have an 'official' language. If you want your state to embrace an official language, then contact your state's elected officials!"

I raised the middle finger at the Anglo as

we walked past his multimillion-dollar classic automobile, and Suiza said, "Our ethical principles embrace diversity and do not incorporate or tolerate discrimination and violent behavior against anyone regardless of race and ethnicity at our financial services empire."

I physically pushed Suiza backward and said, "I don't have a psychological dependence on marijuana and am unlikely to wind up in a drug abuse treatment program for cognitive behavior therapy combined with pharmacological treatment!"

Suiza chuckled, and I said with a raised chin and a Paisley blue bandana worn as a headband, "You can laugh all you want, but I assure you, I would not undergo not one marijuana withdrawal syndrome if I discontinued exhaling marijuana smoke right now."

The brain-released dopamine, a neurotransmitter responsible for producing an emotional response of happiness, made Suiza laugh hysterically. Neurons continued communicating through synapses and making him guffaw. He pounded his chest, then belched with a carbonated soft drink beverage aluminum can in his right hand and stated, "The multinational beverage corporation that produces this soft drink built an iconic American brand acknowledged internationally and is sold in more than 187 countries with more than 20 nonalcoholic brands in the U.S. generating more than $1 billion in revenue every quarter. The beverage company has hundreds of other subsidiary trademarked and licensed beverages around the world."

I wasn't impressed, and said, "And?"

Suiza said, "And . . . The [expletive] beverage company has a leading role in the United States carbonated drink market, and the underlying factor why our financial services firm is involved in its subscription of $150 million 3.5 percent zero-coupon convertible bonds that mature in 5 years."

I walked around a man wearing a midnight blue tuxedo and black silk bow tie procuring a woman wearing a 5-inch miniskirt with removable garters. I observed the procurer slap the woman across her face with intricately designed championship diamond rings on four fingers, and said, "So, in 2000, the zero-coupon notes become due and can be exchanged for stock if the company's shares rise beyond the conversion price."

He said, "Absolutely!"

I asked, "What is your opinion on fixed-income instruments with the lowest bond ratings?"

Suiza's eyebrows closed together like an auditorium curtain and went down, forming vertical wrinkles between the eyebrows of his forehead. He said, "Hmm! That's a good question concerning debt securities."

I responded, "That's why I asked you!"

He replied, "Ratings are shaped by sophisticated evaluations of a corporation's aptitude to pay a stated rate of interest based upon a bond's principal."

A car horn sounded and caught both of our attention. A pearlescent-painted vehicle pulled over, and four desirable women exited the lowrider. The convertible roof was manually unlatched from the windshield and folded into a compartment behind the back seats. Suizo shouted, "Jump in!"

Suiza responded, "We are okay, thanks."

Suizo lifted his car from a four-switch panel mounted on the dashboard and three-wheeled as he made a U-turn at a slow speed to locate the runway models he kicked out of his car.

We stopped at a minimart, and Suiza purchased acetaminophen, an over-the-counter drug used to treat headaches. He lifted his chin up and swallowed both tablets with bottled water while standing in line. Then he slid a consumer debit card through a payment processor at the point of sale and entered his personal identification number to complete the retail transaction. He reviewed the transaction receipt and said, "Benjamin Franklin was right when he said, 'Nothing is certain but death and taxes.'"

I raised one eyebrow higher than the other and stood there dumbfounded. I approached the three-doorway radio frequency electronic article surveillance towers and handed the loss prevention specialist a soft electronic security tag I removed from a boxed good, and said, "I found this on the floor," before stepping outside the minimart. Then I tilted my head back and dropped naphazoline medicine to lubricate both my eyes.

We walked across the street, and Suiza said, "Sales taxes are enforced by the United States federal government at the point of sale of goods and services, then passed onto the state by the merchant."

I interrupted him and said, "I want to learn more about fixed-income instruments with credit ratings less than perfect."

He had an endorphin rush and stated, "Companies with the lowest investment grades are described as high-yield junk bonds and attract contrarian investors, because the bonds carry higher coupon rates."

I knew a thing or two about the bond market and said, "A coupon basically means interest in bond terminology."

He was bug-eyed and said, "You are unquestionably going to be hired into our commercial banking team the day your photo is taken, shaking the chancellor's right hand with a cylinder in your left, and walk offstage in an academic dress to tell the ceremony staff your appellation to acquire your testamur and transcript."

A bald-headed Chicano male in his late 20s standing about 6 feet 4 inches tall, wearing baggy pants with split cuffs and a white T-shirt urinated over a makeshift memorial of candles, and said, "Sorry, I didn't mean any disrespect. An enemy died here, and I am paying homage."

A stocky Chicano male with a shaved head,

thick black mustache and goatee, wearing perfectly creased baggy black shorts and a white tank top, broke away from a group of people with his chin up. He approached us closefisted and stated, "This particular geographic location of 133.2 square miles belongs to Barrio Las Vegas. We don't need an introduction, and we don't need to apologize to anyone."

His associate zipped up his zipper, extended his arm, and said, "Wait! Do you realize who you are talking to? Suizo's brother!"

His eyebrows raised, his eyes widened, and his mouth opened. He said, "We read about you in the financial press all the time."

Suiza reached for a British tan leather business card case lined in suede and handed both of them a 13 diamond-studded business card. He said, "Please, do not hesitate to contact me if you are interested in enrolling in any of our financial literacy programs and are seeking employment."

We continued walking, and Suiza stated,

"The state of California spends millions of dollars on police-led concentrated cannabis eradication operations statewide. According to unanimous resources, your high-volume marijuana plantations are profiting dramatically in a steady state economy and generating hundreds of thousands of dollars in revenue in California."

I said, "What the heck are you talking about?"

I noticed the lip corner tighten and rise on the opposite side of Suiza's face. "You know what I am talking about. Your organization's clandestine pot farms possess illegal pesticides, booby traps, and viciously trained German shepherds. Your associates are legally responsible for the roadside dumping of unwanted gardening tools, sleeping bags, wireless cell phones, candleholders, cultivating gear, irrigation equipment, human waste, and lots and lots of toilet paper," he replied with a wicked smile.

I flex-forward both shoulders with raised

eyebrows in response to his statement, and said, "So?" I watched his eyes widen and mouth open wide.

"So," he said, "It is published in more than 1,300 newspapers, in addition to more than a hundred television and radio stations broadcasting the latest breaking news nationwide."

My smile melted into a frown, and thousands of eccrine sweat glands released a unique mixture of chemical compounds. "No arrests have been made," I said, "And evidence has been handed over to the Bureau of Forensic Services and Federal Bureau of Investigation."

"Are you aware that the city council of Eureka increased the sales tax rate to 5 percent on metered electricity?" Suiza stated.

I became a bit disconcerted after his statement and stated, "Oh, yeah!" I sucked the upper lip vermillion and vermillion lower lip into my mouth.

"Instead of your associates seeing more

black-and-white vehicles with blue and red flashing lights, they are going to see a tax increase on their next energy statement," Suiza stated.

I raised one hand with the thumb positioned in the palm with four fingers extended in the air and said, "Indoor cannabis cultivation businesses use four times more electricity than the average household consumes per month in most cities across the North Continent of the Western Hemisphere, not just Eureka!"

Strip pedestrians inundated a casual dining and drinking destination that Suiza's U.S. national banking and financial services holding company provided merchant account services to. We did not have to book a table in advance, unlike everybody else holding a menu and clinking champagne glasses together. Our server placed a napkin in each of our laps, and I said, "I personally believe the measure is specifically targeting commercial growers, because marijuana garden growing enterprises use high-intensity lights and irrigation systems that imbibe electricity like alcoholics imbibe liquor." I set the 18-carat gold spoon back down and said, "It's a critical revenue source."

"What is?" Austriaco asked.

I gently blotted my mouth with a napkin consistent with the exquisite texture of the tablecloth and stated, "Taxes! I don't know the Senate bill number; however, I do know that existing laws authorize the legislative body of any city to levy a stupid utility user tax on the consumption of gas and electricity. The city council of Eureka enacted the 5 percent utility user tax to preserve balanced budgets to support city services, such as public safety, emergency services, recreation, housing, sanitation, and recycling, but, yeah, what do I know? I am only 13."

Austriaco rubbed the palms of his hands together and said, "Take it easy, no one here is underestimating you!"

I said, "Look! The amount of electricity used by a criminal organization growing marijuana hydroponically in a single 1,500 to 2,000 square foot residence's two-car garage in Eureka is congruent to the electricity consumption of an eminent drug retail chain store. So, from time to time, we use power generators."

The table service was excellent, and the ice-cream sundae I ordered was mouthwatering. Suiza tipped the waitress 25 percent of the restaurant bill, based on the quality of service, and said, "Don't worry, be happy!"

I replied, "I'm not! In fact, the next payment stub we receive from the electric utilities company is going to the recycling bin, because we have over 500,000 pot plants the size of Christmas trees in Mendocino National Forest with a street value of over $25 million."

We lost track of time, and Austriaco unleashed an unprecedented number of unprintable cuss words in the Spanish language. "Let's go," he said. "We are running behind schedule."

A Hollywood actor was arrested by two undercover detectives in untidy clothing posing as street dealers outside the restaurant and took the Hollywood celebrity into custody for purportedly buying spurious heroin, gift wrapped in a balloon he purchased for a measly $20.

We crossed a street bridge and passed East Flamingo Road on Las Vegas Boulevard. Suiza experienced a sharp pain in his lower body muscles and leaned forward rubbing his hands over his quadriceps. "Rod Stewart couldn't have said it better, 'I'm right behind you, win or lose,' so long as I am ambulatory, but you also have to think ahead, and plan for the future. You're already street smart!"

I paused, and said, "Sanitation and forestry city workers can put chemicals on the ground to hinder future marijuana cultivation, and then go about their business each pay period. There are still other rustic areas of the nation where I can sow seeds 1.25 cm precisely into the earth's agricultural soil and transplant pregerminated marijuana plants to raise capital."

Suiza stood at arm's length from a tubular steel utility pool, laughed, and slowly bent his left leg forward with his back straight. He switched legs and repeated the process to stretch his calf muscles.

"You may not be eating a balanced diet," I said. "You need a balanced diet that meets your calorie level and select food with a high-nutrient density."

We looked at each other and laughed until we cried. Foreign particles irritated the mucus membranes of Suiza's nose and triggered sternutation responses clearing his nasal passages. I said, "Bless you!"

Suiza sneezed again and said, "Thanks, fool! The Mendocino National Forest is nearly 364,224 hectares of prime forest land, and undoubtedly, bigger than the state of Rhode Island."

I said, "Most of the pot farms are well hidden and only visible from the air!"

I wanted to backpedal out of the conversation, but Suiza continued rambling and said, "Various law enforcement agencies and comparable competitors are out there."

I couldn't help but laugh and said, "The police department's aviation unit's helicopters are all equipped with forward-looking infrared radar color camera systems with microwave downlinks thermal imaging to discover pot plants on the ground and travel at a maximum speed of about 187 miles per hour at an altitude of 500 feet over their jurisdiction in accordance with Federal Aviation Administration regulations."

We boomeranged to the gleaming aluminum-and-green glass hotel and casino. "Just a minute ago, you looked like a jackpot winner with the top winning lottery ticket, and now you look despondent. What's wrong?" Suiza said.

I was searching for the hotel keycard the desk clerk embedded with a digital code, and stated, "Nevada does not participate in multistate lotteries. Do you want to know something funny?" I asked. "A resident of Tucson, Arizona, chose the pretax cash option of $125 million. Well, a lottery sales representative and district sales supervisor claimed that his wife owns half of the jackpot prize, because Arizona is a community property state."

The bellhop escorted us through the hotel and casino's private entrance. "In California," Austriaco said, "Prize amounts are pari-mutuel!"

The traction steel ropes lowered the car, and the computer turned the electric motor to open the doors to the elevator. The motion sensor system kept the doors from closing as we entered the car, and Suiza said, "I have a better chance of getting struck by lightning twice than winning one of Northern America's largest lottery draw games."

The outer door and indoor of the car opened. A voice said, "¡Échale ganas!"

Suiza glimpsed at the lining of the pant legs and the tortoise shell buttons on the cuff of the 24.9 inch tall dwarf's hand-stitched suit, and stated, "Where the [expletive] did he come from?"

"Maybe out of a perfectly arch-shaped mouse hole cut into the wall," I responded.

"Never mind, forget that I asked," Suiza replied apathetically.

Las Cruces stepped aside, and I inserted the rectangular plastic keycard faceup. The magnetically operated scanner read the coded black stripe and electronically unlocked the door. I turned the handle downward and said, "King Tutankhamun died at age 18. I wonder if I will be remembered after I die."

"Is that what's bothering you?" Suiza stated.

"No! Of course not," I said. "The Money Laundering Suppression Act of 1994 requires law enforcement agencies to provide intelligence ordinarily to the comptroller of the currency and board of governors of the Federal Reserve System to assist in identifying money laundering activities. Other than that, I couldn't be any happier," and quietly closed the door.

Suiza said, "The Bank Secrecy Act requires financial institutions to file currency transaction reports with the Department of Treasury for any sales revenue consisting of more than $10,000, and maintain a paper trail of customers conducting those transactions."

I avoided making eye contact with Suiza, and said, "The Internal Revenue Service requires businesses to request, and report, the taxpayer identification number of people making cash payments above $10,000 on a specified form."

Blanco and Negro activated portable electroshock weapons, and Austriaco vociferated,

"A breach of contract is the most common cause of civil lawsuits and deaths in this country!" He wrapped his right arm around the heavyweight boxer's shoulders and said, "If your cornerman fails to throw in the towel 60 seconds into the first round . . ."

GLOssArY

Alemán–German

Alemania–Germany

Fresno–Ash Tree

Inglaterra–England

España–Spain

El Paso–Passage

Florida–Flowery

San Antonio–Saint Anthony

Colorado–Reddish

Polonia–Poland

Francia–France

Afgano–Afghan

Suiza–Switzerland

Checo–Czech

Irlanda–Ireland

Irlandés–Irish

Austriaco–Austrian

La Brea–The Tar

Santa Fe–Holy Faith

San Francisco–Saint Francis

Africano–African

Fénix–Phoenix

Las Cruces–The Crosses

Blanco–White

Negro–Black

Suizo–Swiss

¡Espere un minuto, por favor!–Wait one minute, please!

Claro que sí, estúpido–I sure do, stupid.

¡Échale ganas!–Work harder!